ISBN 978-1-0980-2933-3 (paperback)
ISBN 978-1-0980-6435-8 (hardcover)
ISBN 978-1-0980-2934-0 (digital)

Christian Faith Publishing, Inc.
832 Park Avenue
Meadville, PA 16335
www.christianfaithpublishing.com

Printed in the United States of America

For Mya
Who brightens our world

Can you find a rainbow on every page?

When I think about Mya
I think of a rainbow
With all of its colors so
bold

If I were so tall
I could reach the sky
I would give her each color to hold

Like her red rosy cheeks
On a cold winter day

Ripe apples we pick from the trees

The nose of a clown,
Balloons at a fair

Her kite flying high
On a breeze.

Fat orange pumpkins at Halloween,
The harvest moon as it rises

Some candy corn.

A new butterfly.
Orange has lots of surprises

The soft yellow down
On a new baby duck
The sun as it warms up the
land

The glitter of stars

Yellow Easter eggs

Castles we build in the sand

Beautiful green
The best color of spring
Fresh grass that feels so good on bare feet

Pine trees that make
The forests stay cool

Or palm trees
That line every street

Under a bright blue Florida sky
The ocean goes on for miles

Bluebirds singing a happy tune.
The color blue
Brings us so many smiles

Purple mountains at sunset
A princess dress to wear

Purple frosting
On her birthday cake

Violets that bloom everywhere

The world is a picture
Of beautiful colors
Painted by God above.
When I think about Mya,
I think of a rainbow
I think about Mya
With love.

About the Author

The author is a Connecticut resident but went to school in Massachusetts where she studied elementary education. She is retired but volunteers in their local thrift shop where they donate to fifteen different charities. She also fills her time by painting seascapes, crafting unusual items, and writing song lyrics. In the past she has taught Sunday school, done a story hour at the library, and worked ten summers as a counselor in a YMCA camp. Reading to her three wonderful children was an important part of their childhood and where their love for reading began. She has always loved writing poetry and short stories. It has always been a dream of hers to write and illustrate a children's book. She hopes many children and their parents will enjoy Mya's Rainbow as much as she has enjoyed creating it.

CPSIA information can be obtained
at www.ICGtesting.com
Printed in the USA
LVHW072206101220
673889LV00012B/225

9 781098 064358